Dear Mom

Volume V

Ukiyoto Publishing

All global publishing rights are held by

Ukiyoto Publishing

Published in 2023

Content Copyright © Ukiyoto

ISBN 9789360164737

All rights reserved.
No part of this publication may be reproduced, transmitted, or stored in a retrieval system, in any form by any means, electronic, mechanical, photocopying, recording or otherwise, without the prior permission of the publisher.

The moral rights of the author have been asserted.

This is a work of fiction. Names, characters, businesses, places, events, locales, and incidents are either the products of the author's imagination or used in a fictitious manner. Any resemblance to actual persons, living or dead, or actual events is purely coincidental.

This book is sold subject to the condition that it shall not by way of trade or otherwise, be lent, resold, hired out or otherwise circulated, without the publisher's prior consent, in any form of binding or cover other than that in which it is published.

www.ukiyoto.com

Contents

Poem by Minnaya34	1
Poem by Mary Grace C. Suplito	6
Poem by Kanishka Agrawal	9
Short Story by Dr. Alokparna Das	14
Poem by Deepika Manju Singh	19
Poem by Jazira Mi	23
Poem by Kanchan Pandey	25
Short Story by Srividya Subramanian	29
Short Story by Monika Arora	39
About the Authors	*52*

Poem by Minnaya34

Carnation

A warmth as perennial and pure as carnation

And the moon's embrace concealed under the sun's ablaze,

Comes from Mom's flames of sacrifice—cape of devotion.

Rough wreaths on my head veiled obscured realisation,

And I was caught lost on trail by soft hand as breeze glaze

A warmth as perennial and pure as carnation.

On its petals that craft my dream and inspiration,

I dance to raving storms, play with winter's craze, with grace

Comes from Mom's flames of sacrifice—cape of devotion.

I tripped during a feat and received laceration

But she stitched it with recognition, paste on my face

A warmth as perennial and pure as carnation.

I was once a kid ire to laws and limitation,
Leave home but always pulled back by force that never chase,
Comes from Mom's flames of sacrifice—cape of devotion.

Floral scent of adolescence, on youth grows passion,
A child blooms into a decent adult yet still trace
A warmth as perennial and pure as carnation,
Comes from Mom's flames of sacrifice—cape of devotion.

Love, Mama

Before flimsy flowers started to wilt and dry,
We took care of them and try
To redeem them on their darkest hour
So their last days there lingers less regret or mournful cry.

Like those chromatic spring bloom, our Mom needs a sunshine,
Go for a healthy walk or a relaxing picnic when the weather's fine;
Might she likes a little time alone in serenity,
Or watch an insightful movie with family while eating nutritious dine.

She may prefer her daughters or sons help her clean their house,
Or give her gift cards to buy beauty products and wear a bonny blouse;
She may be shy to ask for a luxurious royal spa,
Or a sleep in peace without a grouse.

May a grandiose gift of watching sunset on a cruise
Or mountain hiking with her friends or family and drink booze;
A trip to an art museum could be what she wanted
Or growing pots of succulents she would choose.

May we fulfil what our mothers need and desire—
A simple greeting card or do a goal or tasks we both conspire.
A heartwarming letter or a poem is nice and memorable
As long as in our hearts will she discerned our love for her on fire.

"Love, Mama" on a good note transcends warmth on us,
"Love, Mama" with pint of guilt and bottle of regret, pondering why we didn't ask
Or why we didn't set our foot when she didn't give a fuss,
Love Mama for they are our light
And the one who sacrifices a dime bringing us to life.

Poem by
Mary Grace C. Suplito

Consolacion

I miss you every day, I wish you were here.
I hope you can see me, and whisper to me, "Dear."

In my hardest days, I hope I can hug you.
And in my success, I wish I could kiss you.

I love you mom; you are my hero.
In my heart, no one can replace you.

If I will live again and will be asked for one thing,
I will choose to be your daughter again and again.
Dear Mama,

I remember when I got into college, you didn't like the course I wanted to pursue. You said you wanted me to go overseas in the future. But still, I did anyway. I graduated, found my job, and enjoyed it. But as the saying goes, "Mother knows best." Look, mama, I am in Canada, right after I went working in the beautiful island of Bermuda. Yes, I am working overseas and about to finish my diploma course now. I still believe that since you left, you were my guardian angel who looked after me. Look how many blessings I am receiving. I wish you were here to celebrate with me in my failures and success. Thank you for being my backup every time I asked something from the Lord. I miss you, mama. I hope I made you proud. By the way, I saw an advertisement about "Dear Mom Project," and I decided to join because I wanted the whole world to know that I miss you and I love you, Consolacion.

Your daughter forever,

Gracia (this is how you call me, ma)

Poem by Kanishka Agrawal

Lovely Home

Since I was a bundle of nerves
You have been my home.
In a place I had reserved,
I lived in your womb.

I was born through your pain
Yet you didn't complain.
Our first meet and I cried,
You did too but you still smiled.

The world shifted on its axis
And I was stuck in metaxis.
You made me feel safe
And taught me to be brave.

You made me new recipes
And I gave reviews to the best of my ability.
I understood your big words
And you learnt my blabbering.

We played together everyday
Until came a time
You sent me away from you
With tears in your eyes.

Said it's the beginning,
I must explore and learn.
Make new friends and obey my teachers,
I shall now walk and run.

All alone with people unknown,
I kept counting moments.
Till I could be back in your arms,
Not knowing you were there, waiting all the time.

And now that I have grown,
We have distances out of nowhere.

Dear Mom

Out of loop I am thrown
When I don't find you near.

Tests and assignments,
Homework and commitments.
Not that I have forgotten you
But time seems to slip and dent.

When I first fell in love
You knew by my eyes.
I will remember the swans and dove
We talked about till late at night.

You are sending me away again,
This time for college.
Faraway for my personal gain
And I will miss your porridge.

Home for vacation
And you are still the same.
You celebrated me like an occasion
And I am glad I came.

Next time we met,
I had a girlfriend in my arms.
You hugged her before me
And so, everything was calm.

On the day I was set to tie the knot,
You gave me the advice of life.
No matter what happens or not,
We must be happy, not sacrificed.

I have obeyed every word
But I am close to losing you.
Wish we had spent some more time together,
But I will forever love you.

Short Story by
Dr. Alokparna Das

Old and New Memories

Dear Ma,

I know you are unhappy these days; the independent individual in you feels let down due to your dependent and aged self. And though our roles have reversed during the past two years, and I find the role of a caregiver at times a blessing and at others challenging, I, too, miss your former self. Once in a while, I see it again in flashes, when you, even for a few minutes, become the mother and professor "who knows the best" and we get into an argument the way we used to in the past.

I know your once sharp memory is failing due to dementia. So, let me remind you of the wonderful stories that you used to tell me when I was young. When I was scared of darkness and being alone, you told me how you would stay back all alone in a hostel meant for two hundred girls the entire summer vacation, so that you could save the money meant for a railway ticket back home and utilise it in buying books for the next academic session. Books have always been so important for you. It pains me to see that you can no longer read them, though you badly want to. I have learnt from you that one can be a lifelong student. When I was completing my post-graduation and you were writing your post-doctoral thesis, we would both wake up early and sit down to study. During our discussions on politics, you would always relive your memories of Partition. And do you remember the humorous story you read to me years ago about equality in marriage? You had turned it into a play to be enacted by your undergraduate students. I remember the apprehension of your colleagues when you staged it at a theatre competition; after all, the audience may not accept a play in Sanskrit where all the characters were Muslim, they said. I and Baba were, however, confident that you will win the trophy. The play was a hit. The other day, I saw you fondly looking at the photograph of you and your students holding the winner's trophy. I know you miss your teaching and theatre years.

A couple of months ago, my book on the Sun temples in India won an award by Ukiyoto Publishing; you were so happy, trying hard not to forget the title of the book. I want to tell you that my interest in the story of the Sun began when I was in junior school. You had told me the story of a young Aditya, the mischievous son of Kashyap and Aditi, who would want a new room for himself every two months. During summer, he would stay in a room and complain that it was too hot, prompting his doting parents to build another room where it rained for the next two months; he would soon get tired of this and his parents would create a room each for all the seasons—*grishma*/summer, *varsha*/rains, *sharad*/autumn, *hemant*/early winter, *shishir*/winter, and *vasant*/spring. Aditya (Sun) spent at least two months in each of these six rooms. For a long time, I had no idea that this wasn't a myth from the *Puranas* but a story you had created to make the child in me understand the beauty of each season and their relation with the Sun. And that romantic story of a flutist in Bhibhutibhushan Bandyopadhyay's *Meghmallar*, who unknowingly commits a crime, and his atonement, which you read aloud to me and my school friend. It was the first story that made me cry. I am indebted to you and Baba for introducing me to the world of books and storytelling. Every year during Durga Puja, when we would visit the New Delhi Kali Bari, you would buy me books as a Puja gift. I still treasure the Feludas and *Professor Shankus* as well as the abridged versions of classics that you gifted me.

I owe my inclination and training in performing arts to you Ma. I was barely five or six when you would sit through my weekly dance classes and sketch the poses, postures and *mudras* of Bharatnatyam so that I could do my *riyaz* at home.

As I grew up, you made me realise that being independent is not just financial independence. I was and continue to be an average cook—something you tell me often these days. But you know it's not my fault. At a "marriageable age" when many of my friends were joining cooking classes, you had told me that cooking and cleaning are life skills and it's okay if I am unable to impress someone with my culinary skills.

Financial independence for me meant that now the two of us could go on short trips, with Baba managing home. From climbing the caves at Badami in Karnataka to our boat ride on the Ganga to our New Year eve at Sarnath—we have done so many weekend trips across the country, ignoring those who said how two ladies can travel all by themselves.

Like all mothers, who are also teachers, you have taught me so many things. Listening or *shruti* and memory or *smriti* are very important aspects of our traditional knowledge, you had told me. Now that I see you coping with ninety percent hearing loss and a diminishing memory, I realise this everyday. Memory is perhaps the most precious asset that we have and it is our power to not speak but to listen that makes us what we are.

There are days when you seem to be giving up, and it breaks my heart, Ma. Please do not agonise over what you can't remember. We will create new memories, even if they are transient ones. We will travel to new places where we can sit down and listen to not voices but silence. We may not be able to listen to music together anymore, but we can continue to sit together and hear the music that is within us.

Poem by
Deepika Manju Singh

What God Says...

Surrounded by the crowd of fabricated beings,

About Someone, my mind always thinks.

"Someone" who left untimely and early,

I lived a neglected childhood very slowly.

Every day with the failures and trauma of surroundings,
I don't fear her defection, but the motherless boundaries.
Whenever I achieve less success than I deserve,
Recognise, everything will be impossible without who gives birth.

Pretending to be strong and engraved capabilities,
I heard the world is not aware of my insecurities.
Considering me talented and the queen of future,
Everyone creates hurdles, resists my endeavours.
Soon, these emotions won't have ears, voices and expressions,
On the deathbed too, I will think of her and her absence.

I raise my head, glance up at the sky,

A belief that a God exists, I ask him several times,

"How will life be without Mum?

Oh Lord, how will you handle my thoughts?"

He talks to me from within.

"Oh my dear,
Really, how I can handle your thoughts,
Life cannot be lived without a Mum.
Fabrications are the Devil's art,
I'm glad at least you are genuine at your part.
Of course you always think about her,
She is the absolute pinnacle of my created world.
Without mother no childhood you possess,
There is no home, there is no life basis.
Indeed, the problems of life will be raised,
People get courage, ill words they upraise.
But you know, they catch you are more capable,
Dealing with trauma, still a more successful one.
Your emotions will always have voice,
This universe will honour, considering you wise.
Yes, truly said, till death you will realise her absence,
Then I will remind you of my mercy, my compassion.
I understand you completely,
Not because I'm the Creator of yours,
But I feel the same agony you bear.

Be grateful, you have your Lord to complain,

I'm also known as "motherless," have you ever realised my pain?

Many of my humans have her presence, her charm,

Being a God, I have no Mum, but remain to be calm."

Poem by Jazira Mi

Incomparable You

You carried us in your womb,
Barely not a single trace of gloom.
Your eyes spark with charms of joy
Like beaming stars, yet full of chores.
Scent of kindness surrounds the room,
Inner beauty exudes brightness akin to a moon.
Chaos at home seems like battle in the field,
Only you can fix and make something chilled.
Not a day in your life will pass
Without your caring hands ready for us.
You suffer life's ordeals in silence,
Reared up your children with goodness.
Ocean of stars cheering you up
With sparks clapping to raise you up.
Children, each one, longing for you,
Dear mother, this is how much we adore you.

Poem by Kanchan Pandey

I Need You, Mom

Life is a joy and challenges it brings,
But when I suddenly stumble
I need you, mom.
When I don't like things
And I want to grumble;
In all my dawdles and doldrums
And to tolerate my tantrums,
I need you, mom.

When no one believes me
And I want to be heard,
I need you, mom.
When I am restless,
My dreams are endless,
To make me feel proud of my dreams,
And not guilty for my weird whims,
I need you, mom.

We were Papa's princesses and prince,
But how elegantly you've been the queen

With a saree on you and a couple more to possess.
Yet, the magic you spread,
The aura you spewed,
The placidity of your eyes and jingle of your laugh
Could have made no better a better half.

When I often said
Our father is our hero,
Your calm reinforcement
And no jealousy, no insecurity—
So, so, so surprising!
You too ground the mill
And we glorified his will—
Will of endurance, will of resilience, will of sustenance.

We emulated his grit and relished his perseverance,
How naively we forgot we had inherited your penance.
To tell you that you were that unheard hero,
I need you, mom.
To tell you that I wish to tell you
You were my teacher, you've been my friend,

And to tell you that you're my reverend,
I need you, mom.

How foolishly I kvetched you loved them more
When I had been pampered no less than galore.
How villainously silly was I in trying to be evinced
That it was only them with whom you were always convinced.
How could I forget the innumerable moments
That had "you" by me with no judgments.
To thank you for your peerless love,
I need you, mom.

We had bursts of laughter through all thick and thin,
Life was ruthless, life was bountiful.
But, in all her vacillating turmoils, we've been akin,
We fight over rubbish,
We fight like childish.
But, to tell you that we are the brothers and sisters of the millennium,
To tell you that we are the brothers and sisters through all pandemonium,
We will need you, "mom."

Short Story by
Srividya Subramanian

Letter to Mom—My Journey from Womb to Womanhood

Dear Mom,

I know you will be quite surprised to get my letter. I can already hear a hundred sarcastic remarks coming my way. Ha ha! Yes, I am breaking my own rule, or laziness, as you call it, by sitting down with a pen and paper to write.

As you rightly guessed, I have taken up the task of writing to you after long contemplation. I did not write for so long not because there's nothing much to write, but because putting so many emotions into a few sentences is difficult.

However, I wanted this letter to be a surprise gift for you on Mother's Day!

So, here I am! Please put on a brave face till you finish reading my emotional outpourings. And I know you are patient enough to read till the end!

I don't know why but for the past few days, I have been missing you a lot. Of course, I am reminded of you in so many things I do or the happenings around me, but I am not able to control these overpowering emotions any longer.

I long for your presence, your loving and healing touch, and the oft-repeated tales you share without ever getting mad at me for asking you.

I am clueless about where to begin but here it is…

I remember you once told me an incident of how I was while in your womb. You said you used to touch me daily on waking up and wish me "Good morning" and I used to respond by softly kicking your belly. You also told me how I used to cringe if anyone except you or Dad used to touch me then. You labelled me as being intelligent right then, which left me bewildered.

Remember how I laughed at this absurdity?

Now, being a mother myself, I understand your emotions, and you were indeed right! A mother knows how her progeny will turn out to be right from her womb.

When I attained motherhood, I used to be so nervous. I refused to touch Aditi at the hospital, thinking that she might slip from my arms or that I couldn't manage her alone. The new status of "mother" overwhelmed me and I used to cry for hours on end! And you used to just comfort me in silence. No advice, no preaching! How sublime!

Today, I worship motherhood and you!

I don't know if anything exists beyond you.

I remember as a child, I was quite naughty. Once, you told me that I had swallowed a twenty-five paise coin when I was a two-year-old at a function. And all the guests ran helter-skelter in fright trying various methods to get it out of me. Finally, I was fed a lot of bananas and the coin was retrieved in daily ablutions! How hilarious! However, I sensed how worried you had been then.

I also remember my craving for chocolates and sweets, like most children. You were never tired of boasting about how I used to give away whatever I got to my friends or family, including you. But I have known all along, sweetie, how you used to keep your share hidden under my pillow or books for me. You must have sensed my sadness for not having a single treat, ultimately!

There is so much more to tell you, Mom, I hope you are not bored. I can just visualise you holding onto this letter at this late hour. And if I am not wrong, you are reading it in the kitchen, so that Dad doesn't see your tears.

As I speak of your love, I must say I have never seen you pampering me or my sister anytime. We were guided to make our own beds, wash utensils and try our hand at cooking, however tasteless it may turn out to be!

You were so good at stitching fabrics that we hardly had any fancy readymade clothes to wear as children and even as teenagers. We wore handed-over clothes. Though we sulked and protested, everyone admired us as you always saw to it that we were neatly groomed.

Maybe, you wonder why I am repeating this, but I am shocked by the stark differences in upbringing we see in the present generation compared to ours.

Yes, Mom, it is alarming! As a teacher, I realise it even more.

Somewhere, I am also to blame for pampering Aditi and Shreyas. I know you have pointed it out to me several times. But Mom, times have changed so much.

Earlier, we, as kids, never lost our cool at anything you told us to do or did for us. In fact, it was a kind of entertainment for us as there were no other means of entertainment, except for an occasional movie or trip.

Now, technology, the education system and lifestyle have undergone a drastic change. "More" today is "less" tomorrow. Hence, kids are bewildered and are under tremendous pressure to keep up with the competition every single day in order to hold on to their positions in life's rat race. There is nothing personal or private anymore. I have seen youngsters uploading pictures of their routine activities on social media. Can you believe it?

There's not a single soul without a phone in their possession! It has become a dire necessity. Homes which once upon a time used to reverberate with chatter and laughter of their members are now silent while phones which we used only in case of emergency ring all the time. What a paradoxical turn life has taken!

A student who hardly wishes me at school is now my friend on Facebook!

I have been following your advice and trying to infuse liking and respect for our culture, food, and celebrations in Aditi and Shreyas. I also try to see that they learn the importance of keeping up relationships.

By the way, you will be happy to know that Aditi has taken a liking to celebrating the Navratri festival for nine days and nights. She has learned to draw colourful "rangolis" outside our home and even prepare simple yet different *prasad* for nine days. Shreyas plays the violin as she sings different *bhajans* for Goddess Durga.

Hmm ... I can see the wide smile on your face, Mom. Please call her when time permits. I am sure she will be quite thrilled to hear your words of encouragement.

Though everyone around me appreciates me for my values and qualities, I owe every single positive incident that has happened or will happen in my life to you, Mom. You have never preached, only practised. The values you have created in my life by your actions are just so amazing. And that will see me through for a lifetime.

I know that you lay great importance on education. You were the first lady to graduate in your large joint family. I cherish that graduation picture of yours and salute you, my darling!

You have instilled the same strength and qualities of determination in me. I am proud to be a teacher. I take it as a divine calling. I love my students and they reciprocate it in various ways.

I remember that you were unable to work when I was young. But I have grown up with the batches of children who used to come to you for extra classes. How dedicated you were as a teacher!

And when I started going to college, you urged me to take up some of your classes and teach young minds. I agreed then as it was a source of pocket money for me. But over time, it has taught me to be dedicated, time-bound, independent, and work for a better cause.

I remember you saying, "Never ask others to do what you can do yourself. Push your limits! Never borrow money for spending on yourself. Either you earn it and manage your savings to get what you want or let the needs wait till you are competent enough to get them."

As a householder, I realise the tremendous truth behind these words.

Though we belonged to a middle-class family, I have never seen you trying to reach for something beyond your limits. You provided me with the best of everything within your reach, so I was never tempted by anything else, except ice cream!

Mom, I have a little secret that I haven't told you earlier and asked everyone to keep it a secret from you as I wanted to tell you this myself on this Mother's Day!

I am now emerging as a writer. It's been quite some years since I wanted to try my hand at some serious stuff. Now that my children are grown-up and busy with themselves, I took a course in Creative Writing and in no time, pen, paper, word documents, and other media have become my friends!

I write on a variety of topics, in different genres and try my hand at fiction, non-fiction, poetry etc. I am happy to receive appreciation for my writing from various publishers, websites, friends, and relatives. Hope the lazy me can write a novel one day!

I can already visualise your eagerness to read my work. Patience, lady! I will make you read it all when we meet. But right here and now, I have written a poem for you, my precious Mom, from the bottom of my heart!

My Search for You

I search for you, dear Mom,
Among the verdant greens,
The whispering leaves in our garden
Make me believe you have come.

I search for you, dear Mom,
When the fair sky darkens suddenly,
To seek solace in your arms
Which urges me to stay strong.

I search for you, dear Mom,
To show you every award I won
And say how much you belong in every success,
As you made the hard work fun!

I search for you, dear Mom,
For you are my eternal friend and guide
Who just holds my hand in trying times
And helps me swim through the tide.

But today, you aren't around
To listen to my ramblings,
Yet, to say something I can say to none
I search for you, dear Mom!

With this, I end my rather long letter! Please share some of my love and this letter with Dad too! All the sweetness is not for you alone! (Ha! Ha!)

Deepest love to you in this world and beyond!

Short Story by Monika Arora

Thank You, Maa

Childhood is most innocent,

unaware of any sorrows,

playful,

a bit naughty,

every style clear,

nothing artificial,

tender as a flower and beautiful too.

It is like dawn and a feeling of new freshness.

I don't exactly remember when I lived my childhood.

What is sorrow and what is happiness? It is quite difficult to find an answer. It hurts to see others in comfort but we are not happy with our own comforts.

Often those children can do something big in life whose childhood remained full of discomforts.

Whatever is happening in the world is happening inside us too. So, we should seek answers to our queries from our existence and not in this world. We have to encourage ourselves to make efforts and not be dependent on others. It is after getting engrossed in our own journey that you start getting answers from within. The more we peep into the depth of ourselves, the more the replies to our questions get clearer. We shall be able to understand that if we cannot come up to our expectations then how come others can? One should not expect from others, rather one should be a ray of hope for others. When you become one such person only then you attain eternal comfort and feel divine bliss. This is when you realise that the life of everyone is quite similar. Everyone is searching for eternal light. It's of no use to be annoyed by anyone. Everyone is as incomplete as we are. When we attain such a stage, we realise that all are our own.

People appreciate your personality but, frankly speaking, the rightful people for such appreciation are your parents. Their upbringing has made you eligible for appreciation. At times, some incident of your life changes the course of your life. At such times, we curse that pain but, in fact, this only makes us brave. It transforms our lives. When such an incident happens to us, we can't even imagine why it happened to us. The kind of pain inflicted on us is such that our entire life cannot heal its wound. It leaves a hollowness in us which can never be fulfilled in our whole lives. Though difficult, we learn to live with such pain.

Who is a mother? This feeling cannot be described in words. Maa is the greatest wealth bestowed upon us by the Almighty.

Maa is not less than God for the girl in this story. Her mother kept smiling even while enduring sufferings. She kept her sorrows at bay. She fulfilled all my desires though she had no capabilities to do so. She would cry behind the closed doors. She would sleep hungry usually. The girl never saw her mother sleeping. Neither had she seen her mother crying on anybody's shoulder. Whenever she saw her mother, she was standing beside her. She saw her struggling with the time.

Whenever her mother would say, "I am proud of you for being my daughter," a thought would creep in my mind that the name written on the prizes actually belongs to her mother only.

Papa … Papa … Papa … Listen, Papa.

One more, Papa.

Only one more.

Please buy one more fruit, Papa.

The little five-year-old girl was buying all the fruits one by one and was laughing merrily. She would hold the hands of her father and would dance around or would start clapping. She was going to the market holding the hand of her father. She was very fond of visiting the market. Her father would bring her daily, though he could not afford it. He would buy whatever she demanded. Her father was the world's richest father. Her father loved her so much. If she sustained a minor scratch, he would take everyone to the task. Both were enjoying the market when they reached the beetle shop. She asked for a sweet beetle. Papa said, "Oh, yes. Please make two sweet beetles for my daughter."

Suddenly a truck driving rashly on the road hit Papa and threw him on the other side of the road. The little girl could not understand the situation and was wondering where her father went?

The girl cried, "Uncle, where did my father go? How are my fruits scattered here? Please tell me, where is my father?"

The shop owner said, "Where do you live? Please stop crying."

The little girl was lost. The only thing she could see was the crowd. She started collecting the scattered fruits unaware of what had happened to her.

The next morning, she asked her mother, "Why are you crying? Where is Papa? You know, yesterday, Papa disappeared. I know he was playing a prank on me. He was befooling me. When he comes in the evening, you scold him. This is wrong. He should not do such things. Papa is a very bad man."

The mother put her palm on the girl's mouth. "No, daughter, you should not say things like this. Papa is not a bad man." Saying this, she embraced the little girl. After that, neither the mother nor the father was seen in the house. The girl knew that her Papa had met with an accident. He was hospitalised.

After a few months, Papa was brought home. The little girl was overwhelmed. She informed all her friends that her father was coming home.

In the evening, Papa was brought home and was locked in one room. The girl was restricted from going to that room. The little girl was perplexed. She could not understand the situation. She started plotting how she could meet her father.

One day, that girl went to the room of her ailing father and tried waking him up. Suddenly she was slapped on her tender cheeks. She was in a state of shock. Hearing the voice of the slap, her mother came running in the room and embraced her. The little girl sobbed and said, "Maa, Papa is really a very bad man. He slapped me. He is really bad!" She was scared. She had never seen her Papa behaving like this. Papa would keep her close to his chest, then how could he slap her?

Papa had lost his mental balance in the accident. Also, his right hand stopped functioning. Papa would live aloof and mum all the time. He kept on murmuring. At times, he would lose his cool. He would beat mother, break the utensils and, sometimes, would go out of the home without informing anyone. Mother would go berserk. She would find him and bring him home. She would feed him like a kid. All the time, she would serve him. Because of this, Papa started improving. Maa would take care of everybody in the house.

After that incident, the child could not hold the hand of her father but her mother's hand never left hers.

The little girl saw her mother crying and sobbing alone in the room. Maa would conceal her dried tears behind her false smiles and would carry on well with all the relatives.

Maa started working in a factory so that her children could study. She would finish all house chores in the morning before going to the factory. After coming in the evening, she would stitch the clothing of others. She would do even the petty work, whatever she got. She would cook good food and would feed the family with great love. She would also help the neighbours.

One hot day she was returning by bus from grandmother's house. She was carrying two bags and the little girl in her lap. She could not find a seat so she stood near the door. After two hours of standing, she finally found an empty seat. She had unbearable pain in her legs. She felt relaxed when she sat. She had only been sitting for a few minutes when, suddenly, an old lady entered the bus. Maa called that lady very respectfully. "Please, aunty, come here and sit on my seat." She left her seat and helped the old lady sit. Again she was standing.

Auntiji said, "Thanks a lot. I needed this seat very much."

Maa said, "You be comfortable."

The girl was looking at the face of her mother. She wanted to chide her mother, but seeing a smile full of satisfaction on her face, she kept mum. After some time the seat adjacent to Auntiji got vacant but mother offered that too to another lady. At the next stop, again a seat got vacant but mother offered that too to an old man. Maa would often do the same thing. She would never say no to anyone for any work. Though she did not have money in her pocket, she would never say no to anyone.

One day, the girl asked her mother, "Maa, why do you do such things?" Maa replied, "Daughter, I do not have sufficient money so as to help anyone so I help them to earn some good wishes from others. Those wishes would help you in your life. It is said that good wishes are very helpful. What would we carry from this world? So I collect good wishes because they cost nothing. What else can you carry from this world? Life often presents to you two ways: when one would be very easy, but for others you need to have guts to tread it. Very few people dare to tread the tough path. But those who dare the tough path, this world bows to them."

People would laugh at the girl since his father had gone mad but the girl kept moving forward in life in accordance with the teachings of her mother. She would complain to her mother, "Maa, everyone teases me saying that see the daughter of a mad person has come." Maa would tell the girl, "Don't cry, daughter. Tomorrow tell all of them that time will tell you. This girl of a mad man shall do miracles and the whole would witness it. You are not the daughter of a mad man but you are my extraordinary daughter."

She would follow the advice of her mother. Maa used to teach her to move forward and to smile in every circumstance. Maa would say if there is nobody with you then don't be afraid. There is no other company better than ourselves. Maa would often sing, "The train is calling, it is whistling, moving is life and it keeps on moving."

Maa would always encourage to study. During parent-teacher meetings, she would be scared to talk to teachers. But the teachers would always praise the little girl. They would say, "Your daughter is very intelligent. Make her study a lot." Maa would shake her head in affirmation. The girl would stand first in the class. All the teachers of the school loved her. But at the time of final exams of 10th standard, she suffered from typhoid. It was a very severe fever. Maa put bandages of cold water on her forehead. When she felt cold, Maa put a blanket on her. The whole night, Maa remained awake.

The next day, the girl was not fit enough to go to take her exams but mother encouraged her to take the exams saying that her whole year would be wasted. The girl went since her mother insisted. She was taking all the board exams but in the Maths exam of Maths, she fainted for two hours. The teachers tried to revive her and, somehow, she finished forty marks worth of the exam. When she came out of the examination hall, she embraced her Maa and cried bitterly.

The girl said, "Maa, I'll not succeed."

Maa said, "No daughter. Don't say that. The blessings of mother are very powerful. You will definitely get through it." The girl had full faith in her mother. She was declared "Pass" in her 10th exams. Maa was more than happy that day. Maa had linked all her dreams with the future of the girl.

Now, the girl started taking tuitions. She would also help her mother in household chores and other work her mother would do. Maa would always say she was proud of her. "Don't ever let me down." Sometimes she would teach her as a friend but, at times, she would become her grandmother. The girl cleared her 12th exams too. The girl wanted to join a Computer course. All her relatives asked her not to do it but Maa always supported her. Maa borrowed money from her close friend and got her admitted in the Computer course. She would go along with her to the institute and would come back with her. She would sit in the park till the classes were over.

When the girl completed her graduation, proposals for her marriage started arriving. The girl would say no to all the proposals. Somehow she managed to get the consent of her mother and filled the form for post-graduation. But mother always remained apprehensive that the girl might fall in bad company. So Maa started accompanying her everywhere.

One day when the girl returned home, she found her mother weeping in a lonely dark room. She switched on the light of the room and asked, "What happened,

Maa? Why are you crying? Tell me if someone has said anything to you."

Maa said, "Nobody said anything to me. If someone did, would you pay any heed to it?"

The girl asked, "What and who said anything?"

Maa said, "People say that I am allowing you to study further so that I could enjoy the earnings from my daughter. And that is the reason I am not marrying off my daughter."

The girl said, "Since when did you start listening to the talks of the relatives, Maa?"

Maa said, "Daughter, this is society. People don't let you survive if a young daughter is sitting at home. You will understand this when you yourself will become a mother. If a young girl is sitting at home, people start alleging her parents. I have found a boy for you. If you say yes, I shall proceed further."

The girl said, "No, Maa. I cannot say yes to a person who I don't know, I don't love. I cannot make a decision for such a person."

Maa said, "Daughter, it is not bad to love but if you fall in love with the wrong person, your whole life will be ruined. This boy is good. He is educated. You can also continue your studies after marriage. Moreover, how many people I shall keep replying to?"

The girl said, "But, Maa, I don't want to marry."

Maa said, "I have made a decision but if you want to see your mother distressed, then it is your will."

The girl said, "If you have made a decision then what can I say? But I am unable to understand how you've been teaching me to face society but today, you are not listening to me."

The girl consented for the proposal without any further argument.

She remained in that married relationship for a long time but was always thinking about who was right and who was wrong. The girl was not happy with this marriage. She suffered a lot. She was adjusting there for her mother only. She spent twenty-one years with that man who never loved her. For quite a long time, she was under the impression that the man would start behaving. At times she would get annoyed by him but would agree with him later on. Gradually, she started feeling that it was not necessary that the man would come to terms with her. So she started changing herself. The only thing she waited for was the approval of her Maa. The day her mother would approve of, she would free herself from all the relationships because hypocrisy is an illusion and one day it has to end. Facts get exposed one day. It is human nature that a man cannot remain away from oneself for a long time. He cannot remain under a veil for a long time. Maa was worried about what people would say if a married daughter comes back to her parental home. Probably Maa had understood that all the taunts of the people because of which she got her daughter married were present today too. Now Maa had realised the pains of her daughter and she did not want her to bear any more.

So today Maa said, "No more suffering. You start afresh today. You live this life properly and start afresh. You fight with this society. You dream high, make your own home, put a name plate of your own and I am always with you."

The girl was longing to hear these words from her mother for quite some years. She replied, "Thank you, Maa. I was waiting to hear these words for many years. Now you see, your extraordinary daughter would do everything. You are such a wonderful mom. You are my extraordinary mom. Thank you, Maa. Love you, Maa. Proud of you, Maa."

Again the mother and daughter duo were singing, "The train is calling, whistling, moving is life and it is moving."

About the Authors

Minnaya34

Minnaya34 is a writer at heart, a poet in a maze and an aspiring author who loves to make a better and positive change in the world through writing. Writing has always been her home and escape from the harsh and chaotic world so she hopes that her works can shed light to someone in the darkness and give colours to their monochromatic world.

Mary Grace C. Suplito

Mary Grace Constantino Suplito was born in Las Piñas. Graduated from Philippine Normal University with Bachelor's Degree in Secondary Education Major in Filipino. A registered author in National Book Development Board, Philippines. A former teacher at Colegio de Imus, Woodridge College, and Las Piñas East National High School Talon Village Annex. A trainer in Division and Regional competitions in Sabayang Pagbigkas, Reader's Theater, Storytelling, and Speech. She is currently studying at Evergreen College in Toronto, Canada, and taking up Community Service Worker Course. Writing is her passion. Her first written story, "Si Tonyo at Ang Sipit sa Kaniyang Sapatos", is a children's story published in the digital version of Liwayway Magazine in August 2021. "Victor" was published in Luntian - Sixth Issue, 2021. Aside from being a teacher, the most important role for her is being a mother to her four children.

Kanishka Agrawal

Kanishka is a graduate moving towards her Masters with a heart full of passion for writing and learning. Her keen interest in business and fairy tales alike helps her be mature yet keep the innocence in her alive. She is not the one to be withered easily and loves her family unconditionally. She has a book published in her name (*From the Healing Heart*) and several of her pieces have been selected for publishing as a part of an anthology. She looks forward to exploring the world on her terms.

Dr. Alokparna Das

A journalist for thirty years, Dr. Alokparna Das is also a trained musician, having learnt both Hindustani and Carnatic classical styles. Her academic qualification includes Ph.D. in Advertising and three M.A. degrees in English, History, and Mass Communication. She has published more than one thousand articles in newspapers and several research papers in academic journals. She was Senior Editor at India Today, Assistant Editor at The Indian Express, News Editor at The Times of India, and professor at two institutions. Her first book, *Prominent Hindu Deities: Myths & Meanings*, found mention in the Encyclopaedia of Hinduism. Her second book, *Haveli Sangeet*, won the Golden Book 2022 and the Woman Writer of the Year awards. Her third book, *Abodes of the Sun God*, won the Non-Fiction Author of the Year and Golden Book Award 2023. Two of her short stories have won national-level competitions. She has also won the Research Excellence Award in 2020.

Deepika Manju Singh

Deepika Manju Singh is a spirituality practitioner and life motivator. Plant Biotechnologist by profession, she is also a student of theology and explores collaborative religious studies. Compassionate to the plight of Indian farmers, she started her awareness initiative in 2018. Currently, she is writing towards Interfaith Unity, associated with many different religious organisations. She believes in unity and kindness among all beings and serves humanity.

Jazira Mi

Jazira Mi is a published poet, photo enthusiast, and an aspiring novelist. She is a registered writer/author of the National Book Development Board (NBDB), Philippines. Her poetry collection expresses the inner passion and turmoil of intimately intertwined roads of life. *Poems of Life* and *I Do* were published in 2022. *Unspoken Words* will be in the market soon. She is gaining popularity in the international scene and regularly critiques poetry writing contests in an international online platform of aspiring poets. Her works were featured in *Synchronized Chaos*, an e-magazine based in California. She has gained a notable following on Instagram: "My writing Journey- Jazira Mi."

Kanchan Pandey

Kanchan Pandey is a passionate educator, teacher trainer, speaker and writer. Highly self-motivated and zealous learner, transformed from a shy, reticent student to a vibrant, enthusiastic persona, she has been touching lives through her inspiring leadership, motivational talks and seminars and webinars for educators and other young professionals. She is very keen on helping students become confident orators, acquire life-skills apart from making them intellectually competent and helping youngsters to achieve high job satisfaction. She writes on education to bring about innovation in teaching-learning processes. She is presently working as a Principal in a renowned CBSE school near Patna, Bihar and has formerly been a teacher and an HOD English in many reputed schools like St Xavier's High School, Nagpur, Edify School, Nagpur, Nextgen International School, Ongole, Andhra Pradesh and Podar International School, Akola, Maharashtra for about eight years, and an Editor/Author (Academic English Books) at Arihant Publications Pvt Ltd, New Delhi (India) and Rachna Sagar Publications Pvt Ltd, New Delhi (India).

Srividya Subramanian

Srividya Subramanian lives in Chennai, India. She is a teacher by profession and teaches English Literature to high school students. She has written and published her work through anthologies, social media, competitions and the likes in India and abroad. She has won several awards for her writings.

Monika Arora

Monika is a versatile talent exploring all creative fields like writing, painting, creating unique decorative items and making artefacts. She completed her education from Delhi University. She has won numerous accolades, prizes and certificates. She is a benevolent person and has been a reason for improving the lives of many. She's a spiritually strong person who always guides students and people in general. Her ever-present endeavour is to create a society which is as happy as her colours of paintings. She is constantly striving to touch the zenith in every creative pursuit. She has written many stories with heart-touching messages. Some of her works include: "Anjaane Rishte" in *Words; Wreath*, "My Untold Feelings" in *My Feelings on the Paper*, "Broken Without You" in *Summer Waves*, "Beyond Boundaries" in *Wide Awake*, "With You Forever" in *Petals & Chocolates*, "Waves of Love" in *Up Above the World So High*, and "Realisation of Love" in *Nyra*.

www.ingramcontent.com/pod-product-compliance
Lightning Source LLC
LaVergne TN
LVHW041548070526
838199LV00046B/1868